M is for Manners

Abbey & Friends™

I think and do what I hear and see.
Fill my mind to make the best me.™

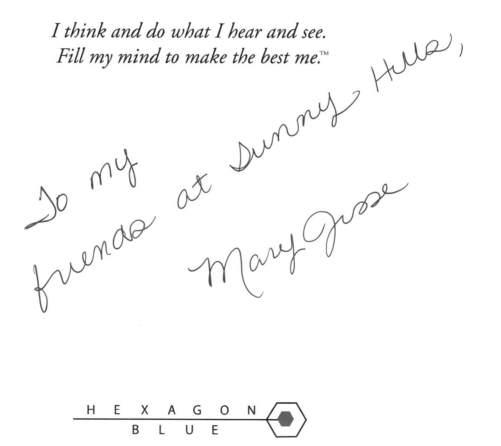

To my
friends at Sunny Hills,

Mary Grosse

H E X A G O N

B L U E

Committed to improving the quality of life™

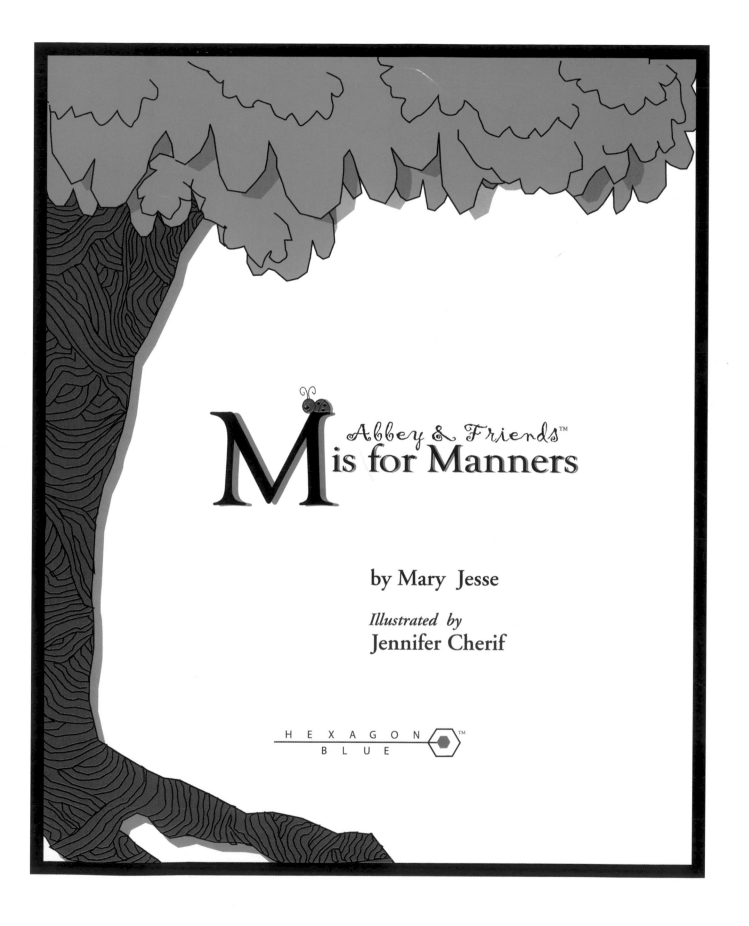

Abbey & Friends™

M is for Manners

by Mary Jesse

Illustrated by
Jennifer Cherif

HEXAGON ™
BLUE

ISBN 0-9729958-0-3

Library of Congress Control Number: 2003105501

Publisher's Cataloging-in-Publication

Jesse, Mary
    Abbey & Friends : M is for manners : featuring Bugsy
/ by Mary Jesse ; illustrated by Jennifer Cherif.
    p. cm.
    SUMMARY: Good manners are highlighted as Abbey
prepares a treat to bring to a friend's house for
dinner. They eat and have fun with their friends.
    Audience: Ages 3-10.
    LCCN 2003105501
    ISBN 0-9729958-0-3

    1. Etiquette--Juvenile fiction. 2. Friendship--
Juvenile fiction. [1. Etiquette--Fiction. 2. Friendship
--Fiction.]   I. Cherif, Jennifer. II. Title.

PZ7.J553172Ab 2003   [E]
                    QB133-1395

H E X A G O N
B L U E   ™

www.hexagonblue.com

*This book is dedicated to
Adam, Amin, Sami, Sofiane, and Zakary.*

*Our children have inspired us to
make this world better.*

*Manners: behavior that shows concern
for other people's feelings.*

M

Hi, I'm Abbey.
I sit in the front row of Mr. Bentley's
third grade class at Greentown Elementary.
I play soccer at recess almost every day
with my best friend, Sarah.
When it rains we play jump rope in the gym.

It's my job to bring in the mail
when I come home from school. "Don't touch the
newspaper!" Max yelled from down the street.
Max always brings in the paper.

Just before the last day of school,
we were invited to eat dinner at Sarah's house.
"Thank you. We'd love to come over for dinner,"
I heard my mom say on the phone.

I knew "we" meant me and my mom and my dad
and my little brother, Max, but *not* our dog,
Jammy.

Max got a puppy for his birthday last year.
"I am going to name him Jammy because
he looks like he is wearing pajamas,"
Max said when he saw the puppy.

My dad said it's Max's responsibility to take care of
Jammy, but sometimes I help out. I don't mind.
It's really kind of fun to take care of Jammy.
He brings us his bowl when he's hungry.

"What shall we bring to Sarah's house?"
Mom said. We always bring a treat
when someone invites us to their home.
"How about grandma's special chocolate cookies?" I said.
I helped my mom bake cookies to bring to dinner.

We mixed flour, butter, sugar, eggs, and CHOCOLATE!
The whole house smelled like warm chocolate.

I told my mom, "I know our friends
usually share the treats with us, but I better taste
one now just in case. Don't you think so?"

"Mom, do I get to taste one, too?"
Max said from the living room.
How did he know I was eating cookies?

Later that evening, we got ready to go
to Sarah's house. I put on my favorite purple shoes
and a matching jacket. Before we went to dinner,
my mom reminded us to use our "best manners."

You know, I've never been asked to use my worst
manners anywhere!

We didn't want to keep our friends waiting,
so we left right on time. I waved goodbye to Jammy.
He was peeking through the hole in our fence.

We talked in the car about greeting people
and looking in their eyes when you talk to them.
I thought about all the people I see in the day,
and whether I looked at their eyes.

"Hi, glad you could make it," said Sarah's mom.
She smiled when she saw the cookies we brought.
Everyone said hello to everyone.
Sarah's mom hugged me and Max.

We had a little time before dinner,
so we decided to play some games.
Since we were her guests, Sarah said we
could pick out the game and even go first.

That was really nice.
I think I'll have guests go first at my house.
No wonder Sarah's my best friend.

Soon, we were called to eat dinner.
We put the games away and headed upstairs.
Of course, we each stopped at the
bathroom to wash our hands before dinner.

Mmmm, they have that foamy soap
that smells like strawberries.
I think I better wash my hands twice.

Everything at the table looked so good.
I tried a little of each dish and decided
I liked the mashed potatoes best.

Our parents talked a lot,
and Max kept his eyes on the cookies.

I waited for a quiet moment then asked,
"Could you please pass the potatoes?"
"Certainly, here you go," said Sarah's mom.

"I better not have too much," I thought.
I needed to save room for those cookies.

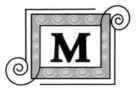

I really didn't like the peas and almost said,
"Yuk! Those are really icky."
Then I remembered it isn't polite to make
comments like that at the dinner table.

Those icky peas stared right at me, but
I just looked the other way.

M

I smiled at the mashed potatoes.

After dinner, everyone helped clear the dishes.
Sarah's mom looked really happy.
She brought out the cookies and everyone smiled.

I think they tasted just a little better
at our friend's house.

Finally, it was time to go home.
I was sad to leave my friends, but didn't feel bad
at all about leaving those peas behind.
We thanked our friends as we said goodbye.

What a fun time we had!
I heard Sarah's mom say,
"Your children have such nice manners!"

I told Max that Sarah's mom said
we had nice manners.
He acted like it was no big deal, but
I could tell by the look on his face
it made him feel good.

My teacher looked a little surprised
when I walked in the class,
looked him straight in the eyes and said,
"Good morning, Mr. Bentley!"
Then he surprised me with a big smile,
"Good morning, Abbey!"

Was he happy about the greeting or because
it was the last day of school?

To our friends,
Thanks for inviting us to
dinner. We had a terrific
time!
Love,
Abbey & Max

Abbey's Manners Tips

- ✔ Say "Thank You" when you are given something.
- ✔ Be on time, especially if you are meeting someone.
- ✔ Say "Please" when you ask for something.
- ✔ Help clear the dishes after meals.
- ✔ Bring a treat when you're invited to eat at someone's house.
- ✔ Greet people when you see them.
- ✔ Say "You're Welcome" when someone thanks you.
- ✔ Talk politely during meals.
- ✔ Be nice to people.
- ✔ Help your family members.
- ✔ Let your guests go first.
- ✔ Wash your hands before eating.
- ✔ Look people in the eyes when you talk to them.
- ✔ Send thank you cards to show appreciation.
- ✔ When other people are talking, wait to talk.
- ✔ Share with others.

(All these tips are in the story somewhere, except one...)

Here are your FREE bookmarks!

Fold line

Cut along the dotted line.

M is for Manners

Abbey & Friends™

I think and do what I hear and see. Fill my mind to make the best me.™

www.hexagonblue.com

Abbey™ Friends

Read aloud and leave a lasting impression to help any child live a better life.™

www.hexagonblue.com

This is where you stopped

www.hexagonblue.com

This is where you stopped

www.hexagonblue.com

Look for authentic
Abbey & Friends™
products
www.hexagonblue.com

Fold here

This is where you stopped

Hi, I'm Abbey.
I sit in the front row of Mr. Bentley's third grade class at Greentown Elementary.
I play soccer at recess almost every day with my best friend, Sarah.
When it rains we play jump rope in the gym.

It's my job to bring in the mail when I come home from school. "Don't touch the newspaper!" Max yelled from down the street. Max always brings in the paper.

Sample (not to scale)

The End